Little Boo

Stephen Wunderli

ILLUSTRATED BY Tim Zeltner

HENRY HOLT AND COMPANY • NEW YORK

Henry Holt and Company, LLC
Publishers since 1866
175 Fifth Avenue
New York, New York 10010
mackids.com

Henry Holt® is a registered trademark of Henry Holt and Company, LLC.
Text copyright © 2014 by Stephen Wunderli
Illustrations copyright © 2014 by Tim Zeltner
All rights reserved.

Library of Congress Cataloging-in-Publication Data
Wunderli, Stephen.
Little Boo / Stephen Wunderli ; illustrated by Tim Zeltner. — First edition.
pages   cm
Summary: A pumpkin seed tries unsuccessfully to be scary until it grows into a pumpkin and Halloween arrives.
ISBN 978-0-8050-9708-5 (hardcover) — ISBN 978-0-8050-9709-2 (e-book)
[1. Halloween—Fiction. 2. Jack-o-lanterns—Fiction. 3. Pumpkin—Fiction. 4. Seeds—Fiction.
5. Growth—Fiction.] I. Zeltner, Tim, illustrator. II. Title.
PZ7.W96375Li 2014   [E]—dc23   2013030796

Henry Holt books may be purchased for business or promotional use. For information
on bulk purchases, please contact Macmillan Corporate and Premium Sales Department at
(800) 221-7945 x5442 or by e-mail at specialmarkets@macmillan.com.

First Edition—2014
Book designed by Véronique Lefèvre Sweet
The artist used acrylic on plywood and a unique combination of stains
and glazes to create the illustrations for this book.
Printed in China by Toppan Leefung Printing Ltd., Dongguan City, Guangdong Province

3   5   7   9   10   8   6   4   2

To all the Little Boos who want to be big—
Be patient, keep trying, and one day you will
be more than you can imagine.

This book is for Rylie, who loves
to watch the garden with Grandpa.
—S. W.

To Griffen
—T. Z.

The wind blew, the leaves fell,
and a tiny seed hid in the garden.

"Boo," the seed said to
a leaf rolling by.

"You're not scary at all,"
the leaf said.

A grub was burrowing in the soil nearby.

"Boo," said the seed.

"I'm busy," said the grub.

The seed sighed. It began to get cold.

A snowflake fell close to the seed, then another, and another.

"Boo. Boo. Boo," the seed said.

"There's more of us than you," the snowflakes whispered back. "Why would we be scared of you?"

Poor seed.

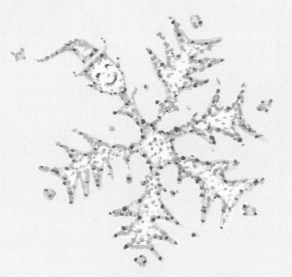

"It's not time for scaring," the wind said. "Not yet. Be patient. You'll be scary soon enough."

"I want to be scary now," the seed said, trying to make himself big.

"Just wait," the wind whispered, carefully blowing soil over the seed to keep him from the cold.

The seed sighed one last time and finally fell asleep.

"Boo," he said in his dream.

It was a very long sleep, and when the seed awoke, the air was warm above him. He reached for it, reached and reached until he could feel it.

"Ahh," the seed said. "Time to get back to scaring."

The seed was growing into a tender little sprout.

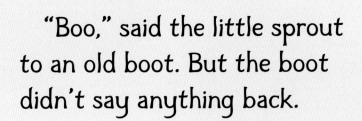

"Boo," said the little sprout
to an old boot. But the boot
didn't say anything back.

"Boo," he said to a shovel.
But the shovel was silent.

"Boo," said the little
sprout to a watering can.
But the watering can didn't
say a word either.

So the young little sprout
decided to keep growing.

The wind came by for a visit. "Boo," said
the sprout, who was now a little plant. He
was proud of how big he had gotten.

"Not today," said
the wind. "But soon . . .
soooooooooon."

The little plant kept growing, and sometimes tried to scare the bucket and the bees and a grasshopper.

"Boo. Boo. Boo," he said.

But none of them were even the least bit afraid.

So the plant that began as a seed grew and grew and grew. Soon little orange flowers appeared. *Flowers aren't very scary,* he thought. But then the flowers fell away and little green fruit began to grow. They grew fast.

"Can I boo now?" the plant asked the wind.

"Not quite yet," the wind said.

One round green fruit grew much bigger than the others, and then it turned orange . . . a pumpkin!

"Boo," the pumpkin said to the hands that picked it, but they weren't scared as they carried the pumpkin to the house.

The wind shut the door behind them. "I'll be right here," the wind said.

Darkness crept in
above the trees.

There was no moon.
A single candlelight
appeared in the night.

"BOO!" said the pumpkin
that was now a jack o'lantern.

"Yeow!" said the cat.

"Good scaring!" said the wind. "Do it again."

"BOOO!" said the jack o'lantern.

"AAAAAAAAAhhhhhhhh!" screamed the goblins.

"Wooooooooooooooooeeeeee!" said the wind, whirling around the bare trees and stirring up the leaves. "What wonderful scaring!"

"Thank you," said the jack o'lantern who used to be only a seed.

"Boo!

"Boo!

"BOO!"

And the light from the jack o'lantern's grin flew over the trees and spread across the night.